EGMONT

We bring stories to life

First published in Great Britain 2017 by Egmont UK Limited
The Yellow Building, 1 Nicholas Road, London W11 4AN

Adapted by Tallulah May

Illustrations by Steve Kurth, Andy Smith, and Chris Sotomayor
Directed by Jon Watts
Produced by Kevin Feige and Amy Pascal
Based on the screenplay by
Jonathan Goldstein & John Francis Daley and
Jon Watts & Christopher Ford and
Chris McKenna & Erik Sommers

© 2017 MARVEL © 2017 CPII

ISBN 978 1 4052 8824 8

67835/1

Printed in Italy

MARVEL
SPIDER-MAN
Homecoming

MEGA MOVIE
STORYBOOK

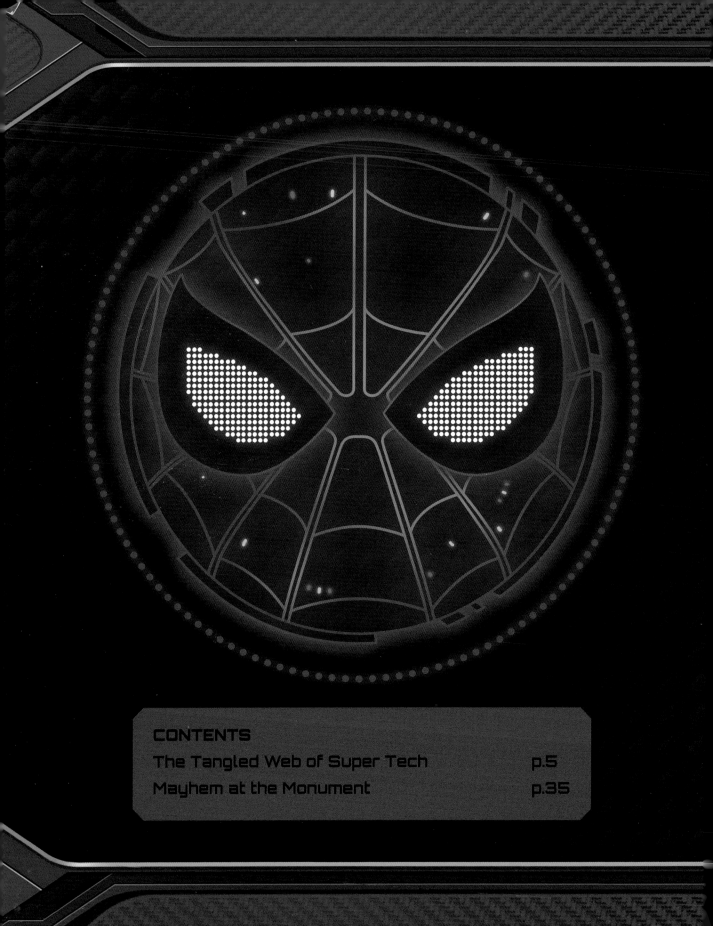

CONTENTS

MARVEL
SPIDER-MAN
Homecoming

THE TANGLED WEB OF
SUPER
TECH

Peter Parker is coming off the most intense experience of his life – helping Iron Man fight in the Avengers' Civil War as the high-flying Spider-Man.

Now he's working on becoming a fully-fledged Avenger, although he has a long way to go. Luckily for Peter, Tony Stark, aka Iron Man, is helping him out. So Peter gets rides in the Stark Industries limo and forms a little bit of a bond with Happy Hogan, who is honestly never that happy.

Being friends with Tony means Peter has access to some awesome technology, including – one day, maybe – the state-of-the-art Avengers Tower, which soars over the New York City skyline.

Peter has come a long way from his original homemade suit. There's not a whole lot a high-school kid with a limited amount of money and sewing experience can piece together in secret, so it wasn't the most stylish costume in the world. Except for the hood... that was awesome.

But he had made custom goggles to perfectly suit his powers. They helped Peter focus when the action around him picked up speed.

His web shooters are his own design, and he makes his own super strong webbing from scratch, usually under the table in his chemistry class.

The new suit comes straight from Tony Stark. It's high-tech, and he even kept the signature red and blue colours. *These* eyepieces react to Peter's face and outside factors, giving his mask some flexibility in a fight.

There are a lot of features to discover about any piece of Stark tech, and Peter's just the science whiz to do it.

What good is a spider without any webs? Spider-Man's webs are perfect for catching fleeing thieves, trapping muggers until the police arrive, or swinging through the city.

Peter's webs dissolve in about an hour. So even bad guys won't be stuck to pavements and lamp posts forever.

Something Peter can do whenever he wants — in or out of his costume — is wall-crawling, one of Spider-Man's most useful abilities. He can use it to sneak up on bad guys, or even just creep them out. It's not every day you see a Super Hero hanging out on the ceiling.

He can also get to tall rooftops — perfect for surveillance and web-swinging. It's important that his costume doesn't get in the way of his natural wall-crawling, and his designs make sure he's able to scale sheer walls with no problem.

Other tools at Spider-Man's disposal are his tiny Spidey trackers. These little robotic spiders can cling to anyone, and avoid detection. All Spidey has to do is check on his holographic map, and he knows exactly where a mark is hiding.

Using all this amazing technology, Spider-Man can track down basically anyone, and swing in to save the day. Just ask the German chancellor.

With his friend Ned's help, Peter is even able to unlock upgrades to the suit Tony gave him to use. Tony had put more technology behind some safety measures, but Peter and Ned are good enough with tech to access the super-secret features.

For instance, the suit now includes high-tech imaging software! Spider-Man's suit has an advanced AI that helps him through different dangerous situations.

When there are people in danger, this software lets Peter know exactly where they are, how many people could be hurt, and how to best tackle the problem.

All the tech in the world doesn't mean Spider-Man can take on crime alone. Luckily, every once in a while, his mentor, Iron Man, is around to help him out of particularly tough jams.

But Tony Stark and Peter Parker aren't the only ones in the world who know how to use cutting-edge tech....

Adrian Toomes used to run a cleaning crew that cleaned up particularly huge messes – like the rubble from the end of the Battle of New York, when the Avengers assembled for the first time and pushed back the Chitauri invasion of Earth.

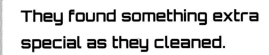

They found something extra special as they cleaned.

Working with a man known as the Tinkerer, Adrian was able to convert some technology from space into a dangerous new weapon that could take out Spider-Man for good.

The Tinkerer used to salvage with Toomes, but since they lost their valuable contracts to the government, he's been helping out on other projects. He's a technical genius.

He helped outfit Toomes's crew with powerful new gear. These gauntlets transform a normal guy like Herman into the Shocker — turning ordinary punches into super powered assaults capable of knocking even Spider-Man out of a fight.

Of course, Toomes saved some of the best stuff for himself, robbing even more tech from delicate government shipments, and getting the better of Spider-Man more than once.

With razor-sharp talons and enormous mechanical wings, the Vulture is incredibly formidable because of his tech. He has enhanced vision thanks to his eerie, glowing green eyes.

Peter knows he's in for a fight, especially when the bad guys have equipment just as impressive as his. But at the end of the day, he has the determination to come out on top. After all, he's the amazing Spider-Man!

MARVEL
SPIDER-MAN
Homecoming

MAYHEM AT THE
MONUMENT

After school, Peter Parker is Spider-Man —
a web-swinging, wall-crawling, crime-fighting
Super Hero. But at Midtown High School of
Science & Technology, he's just a kid... a kid
with the secret power to jump out of the way
of speeding cars!

At school, only one person knows that Peter is secretly Spider-Man. That person is Peter's best friend, Ned. Sometimes Ned is even more excited that Peter is Spider-Man than Peter is!

Usually fighting crime is awesome! But sometimes being a Super Hero gets in the way of life... and crushes.

Liz is the Academic Decathlon team captain, and she wants Peter to join them for the national competition in Washington, DC. Even though Peter really wants to go, he has to stay in New York. What if the Avengers call and he's not there to help?

BOOM!

One night, while wearing his Spider-Man costume, Peter hears an explosion. He climbs to a rooftop to find out what's going on and sees a giant purple light arcing across the sky.

The light crashes down a few miles away. Peter has seen light like that before. He knows it's alien technology — very dangerous alien technology.

At the crash site, two guys are piling advanced weapons into a van. When they see Spider-Man, one crook pulls out a gun. *THWIP!* Spider-Man quickly webs the gun to the crook's hand. Things seem to be under control when...

WHAM! The other guy punches him with some sort of high-tech gauntlet. Spider-Man gets shocked and knocked back about ten feet in the air. He smashes into a nearby pillar!

With Spider-Man dazed, the men jump inside the van and take off down the street. But Peter isn't going to let them go so easily.

THWIP! THWIP! He uses his webs to attach himself to the van doors. As they zoom around a corner, he loses his grip. The men get away, but the tight turn sends one of their alien weapons flying out of the van.

The next day, Peter brings the strange thing to class. Maybe he and Ned can figure out a way to open it. At first the weapon won't budge. Then, with a *POP*, it comes loose.

Peter and Ned sneak into the science lab that night to investigate, but two men from the van break in to the school looking for the weapon. Peter and Ned just barely manage to hide. Peter quietly shoots a Spidey tracker at one of the men as they leave — now they can track where the men are going and who they work for.

They track the bad guys to a city near Washington, DC. Looking at the map, Peter gets a great idea. The decathlon is taking place in DC. If Peter joins the team, he'll get a free ride to the bad guys' evil lair!

In preparation for the trip, Ned helps Peter, but he's also worried for Peter's safety. Ned wonders if bursting into a secret lair is the best idea.

In DC, Spider-Man sneaks away from the decathlon team to track the men from the van. But when he finds them, they quickly trap him in a cargo container filled with even more alien technology.

Trying to escape, he asks his upgraded talking suit about the alien weapons. She explains that if the energy source for the weapon is damaged, it will explode.

Oh no! Peter realises he left the other weapon with Ned! *Not* good! Ned is at the Washington Monument with the rest of the decathlon team. It could explode at any second and destroy everything, and Peter is too far away to warn him. He's got to get there quickly!

Finally! Peter makes it to the Washington Monument.

Tourists and school buses are everywhere. Peter can't see his classmates, so he makes a mad dash for the tall, white monument, running and leaping as fast as he can.

He spots one of his classmates, Michelle. In his best, deepest Super Hero voice he asks her, "Where is your class?"
She points at the monument, but before she can say anything else...

FWA-BOOM! An explosion rocks the building.

The tech in Spider-Man's suit tells him that the explosion came from an elevator at the top of the monument. That's where his friends will be. Spider-Man starts climbing up the monument as fast as he can. He has to get to them before the elevator falls!

At the top he hears the whipping of helicopter blades. The police in the helicopter think he's attacking the monument! But there's no time to explain.

The tech in his suit counts down the seconds until the elevator falls. "Five seconds."

Just in time, Spider-Man crashes through the glass of the observation deck and into the Washington Monument.

THWIP! He manages to fire his web down the elevator shaft and catches it before it falls. Slowly, using his superhuman strength, he's able to hoist it back up.

Without warning, the support web snaps, and Spider-Man is jerked into the elevator shaft. They're going down again!

Thinking fast, Spider-Man gets inside the elevator and shoots another web straight up, to the top of the elevator shaft. Using his legs to brace himself, he's able to stop their fall.

"I knew you'd make it," says Ned as Spider-Man secures the web to the elevator. He helps everyone climb through the hole in the roof to safety. Liz is the last one Spidey has to rescue.

The elevator roof starts to groan. Then, suddenly, the roof snaps off completely. Liz is falling! *THWIP!* Spider-Man quickly shoots another web to catch her.

Everyone is finally safe on the ground. But Spider-Man can't stay to talk. He gets nervous around Liz and doesn't want to accidentally reveal his secret identity. Plus, he's got more people to save. After all...

...he's **SPIDER-MAN!**